SandCastle

Healthy Habits

Taking Time to Relax

Mary Elizabeth Salzmann

Consulting Editor, Diane Craig, M.A./Reading Specialist

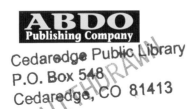

Published by ABDO Publishing Company, 4940 Viking Drive, Edina, Minnesota 55435.

Printed in the United States.

Credits
Edited by: Pam Price
Curriculum Coordinator: Nancy Tuminelly
Cover and Interior Design and Production: Mighty Media
Photo Credits: BananaStock Ltd., Brand X Pictures, Comstock, Digital Vision, Image Source, Stockbyte

Library of Congress Cataloging-in-Publication Data

Salzmann, Mary Elizabeth, 1968-
      Taking time to relax / Mary Elizabeth Salzmann.
          p. cm. -- (Healthy habits)
      Includes index.
      Summary: Explains in simple language the importance of relaxation to maintaining good health.
      ISBN 1-59197-555-7
       1. Relaxation--Juvenile literature. [1. Relaxation.] I. Title.

RA785.S257 2004
613.7'9--dc22
                                                                                2003057794

SandCastle™ books are created by a professional team of educators, reading specialists, and content developers around five essential components that include phonemic awareness, phonics, vocabulary, text comprehension, and fluency. All books are written, reviewed, and leveled for guided reading, early intervention reading, and Accelerated Reader® programs and designed for use in shared, guided, and independent reading and writing activities to support a balanced approach to literacy instruction.

Let Us Know

After reading the book, SandCastle would like you to tell us your stories about reading. What is your favorite page? Was there something hard that you needed help with? Share the ups and downs of learning to read. We want to hear from you! To get posted on the ABDO Publishing Company Web site, send us e-mail at:

sandcastle@abdopub.com

SandCastle Level: Transitional

Taking time to relax
is a healthy habit.

Relaxing means doing something calm that you enjoy.

Relaxing gives your mind and body a break from the busy parts of your day.

When you relax, you can forget about your problems for a little while.

Val and her mom play dominoes.

Joel likes to do jigsaw puzzles.

Patty likes to read stories.

Andy likes to play checkers.

Faith likes to listen to music.

What is your favorite way to relax?

Did You Know?

The oldest known set of dominoes was found in King Tutankhamen's tomb and is more than 3,000 years old.

The world's largest jigsaw puzzle was put together in France in 1992. It was 12,401 square feet.

The game checkers is called **draughts** (pronounced **DRAFTS**) in England.

The Walkman was invented in 1979.

Glossary

checkers. a game for two people played with small disks on a checkered board

dominoes. a game played with flat, rectangular tiles that are divided in half with zero to six dots on each half

habit. a behavior done so often that it becomes automatic

healthy. preserving the wellness of body, mind, or spirit

jigsaw puzzle. a puzzle with many small, irregular pieces that are put together to form a picture

problem. a situation that needs deep thought in order to reach a solution

About SandCastle™

A professional team of educators, reading specialists, and content developers created the SandCastle™ series to support young readers as they develop reading skills and strategies and increase their general knowledge. The SandCastle™ series has four levels that correspond to early literacy development in young children. The levels are provided to help teachers and parents select the appropriate books for young readers.

Emerging Readers
(no flags)

Beginning Readers
(1 flag)

Transitional Readers
(2 flags)

Fluent Readers
(3 flags)

These levels are meant only as a guide. All levels are subject to change.

To see a complete list of SandCastle™ books and other nonfiction titles from ABDO Publishing Company, visit **www.abdopub.com** or contact us at:

4940 Viking Drive, Edina, Minnesota 55435 • 1-800-800-1312 • fax: 1-952-831-1632

J.2